Mele Kalikimaka

The Tradewinds Series

Porch Swing Girl
Sand Castle Dreams
Mele Kalikimaka
Barefoot Memories

Mele Kalikimaka

A Christmas Novella

By Taylor Bennett

Mele Kalikimaka
Published by Mountain Brook Ink
White Salmon, WA U.S.A.

The website addresses shown in this book are not intended in any way to be or imply an endorsement on the part of Mountain Brook Ink, nor do we vouch for their content.

This story is a work of fiction. All characters and events are the product of the author's imagination. Any resemblance to any person, living or dead, is coincidental.

Scriptures taken from the Holy Bible, New International Version®, NIV®. Copyright © 1973, 1978, 1984, 2011 by Biblica, Inc.™ Used by permission of Zondervan. All rights reserved worldwide. www.zondervan.com The "NIV" and "New International Version" are trademarks registered in the United States Patent and Trademark Office by Biblica, Inc.™

ISBN 978-1-953957-14-6

The Team: Miralee Ferrell, Nikki Wright, Cindy Jackson
Cover Design: Indie Cover Design, Lynnette Bonner Designer

Mountain Brook Ink is an inspirational publisher offering fiction you can believe in.
Printed in the United States of America

*To anyone who has felt the pain
of loss during Christmastime—
You are not alone*

Acknowledgements

When I first had the harebrained idea for this little story, I knew absolutely nothing about it, save for the fact that I desperately wanted to combine two of my greatest loves—Olive (plus the rest of the *Tradewinds* gang) and Christmas. At first, writing it was something fun. I wasn't exactly sure what I was going to *do* with the story once it was finished.

And then my amazing editor stepped in. When I told her about how hard I had fallen for this short, simple Christmas novella—and how desperately I wanted to share it with my readers—she agreed to publish it. So, Miralee Ferrell, my first thank-you (plus a mound of *Tutu*'s famous macadamia nut shortbread) goes to you. For your editing expertise, your incredible kindness, and your willingness to go along with my crazy writing schemes, you have my unending appreciation. (Seriously, friends—I've met a lot of people in "the biz" in the last few years, and none of them can compare to this publishing powerhouse. If you're an author, you *need* a Miralee in your life!)

Thank you also to Sonya Downing and Jenny Mertes for your incredible help during content edits/proofreads, and for your warm encouragement and virtual hugs. I'm toasting you with my hot cocoa.

Special thanks and an extra slice of macadamia nut pie to my mom and grandmother, who inspired many of the traditions mentioned in this book. Though my grandma is no longer with us to read Olive's story, my mom read through my story not once or twice but approximately *ten million* times as I edited and revised it. Mom, you're the best!

And, to all of my Porch Swing Girls—the lovely ladies who have stuck by me through thick and thin throughout countless launches, brainstorming sessions, etc.—I give you all of the drummers drumming, golden rings, and calling birds in the world. (Plus everything else from the other nine days.) I don't know what I would do without your sweet support and encouragement. You're the best!

Chapter One

"MELE KALIKIMAKA IS THE THING TO say on a bright Hawaiian Christmas Day..." The chorus of the old Bing Crosby song pours from the speakers inside Foodland for what must be the millionth time since Gramma and I stepped inside to begin our shopping.

"Can't they play anything else?" I lift my hands, as if to cover my ears. "If they keep going like this, I'm going to be sick of Christmas before Thanksgiving weekend is over."

Gramma chuckles. "Christmas over here is a little different. You'll get used to it. Can you grab me a pineapple?"

"Sure." I walk over to the box and grab the biggest spiky, yellow fruit I can find, Gramma's words weighing down my feet—and my heart.

She's right, you know. A snarky little voice I recognize from last summer whispers in my ear. *This Christmas is going to be way different. You're in Hawaii, for one—and don't pretend you've forgotten about—*

"Shut up." I spit the words out under my breath as I tromp back toward Gramma's shopping cart.

"Pardon?" Gramma slides her glasses onto her nose and peers at her list.

"Sorry, Grams. Just...talking to myself." My cheeks grow warm—I must be flushing the color of a poinsettia. So now I'm talking to myself. Maybe the craziness of the last six months has finally made me crack.

Gramma glances up, her gaze softening, and she steps forward to give my arm a squeeze. "Is everything okay?"

"I guess." I breathe deep as we start toward the bakery section. "It's...I dunno. Macie's all excited about going to church on Christmas Eve and writing her letter to Santa, and all I want to do is crawl into a hole and—hibernate."

Gramma smiles, the weakest, saddest smile I've ever seen. Her eyes twinkle, but I doubt it's because she's happy. How can she be when her own son-in-law couldn't find the time to call and wish us a happy Thanksgiving on Thursday? When I'm moping around like it *isn't* the most wonderful time of the year. When, for the first time ever, Mom wasn't here to celebrate Thanksgiving with us.

My eyes burn with unshed tears, but Grams doesn't offer any words of consolation or wisdom—only another shoulder squeeze as we travel further into the depths of Foodland. We make quick work of the lengthy shopping list, but it isn't until we're driving back home that Gramma opens her mouth to speak again.

"Your mom loved Christmas, you know."

"You don't say." My gut twinges as a vision of my mom, all decked out in her Mrs. Claus apron and elf hat, leaning over the oven to take out a batch of ginger Christmas cookies, accosts my memory. "It was her favorite time of year." Mine too.

But now she's *gone, and* I don't even know what Christmas is without Mom. Day-to-day life is hard enough, but now? With sleigh bells ringing and choirs singing? I lean back against the car seat and sigh.

"She was such a kind soul, especially around Christmas. Did you know she mailed me a Christmas stocking every year? It was different every time, but it was always filled with goodies and a note." The usual light in Gramma's eyes dims. "I have to keep reminding myself that there won't be any note this year."

My heart crunches in my chest—how can I be so

selfish? Only worrying about myself and my own woes, when the people around me are missing Mom too? I twine a finger around my seashell necklace and stare out the window at the pounding surf—no snowflakes or silver bells here—as we turn onto Gramma's street.

"I can't imagine how tough this must be on you and Macie." Gramma pulls into the driveway and puts her rusted old station wagon in park, then reaches over and rests a hand on my knee. "Remember—I'm here for you whenever you need to talk."

"Thanks, but I'm okay." I unfasten my seatbelt and straighten my spine. Maybe, if I tell myself that enough times, I'll actually believe it. "It's Macie I'm worried about."

My six-year-old little sister has handled Mom's death surprisingly well, but everything seems tougher during the holidays. Especially since Dad is...well, Dad.

"Try not to worry, Olive." Grams gives my hand a pat before opening her car door and climbing out. "God gave us this season so we can celebrate the birth of His son and remember the promise that we will *all* someday be united with Him in Heaven."

"I know." I step onto the driveway and reach back into the car for an armload of groceries.

But that doesn't make it any easier. That little voice hums a mournful version of Elvis's "Blue Christmas" in my ear as I climb the front porch steps, and I can't help but agree with it.

"Olive!" Macie jumps up from her spot on the couch next to Jazz, my best friend, the second I walk in the front door. "Jazzie taught me how to say Merry Christmas—but in Hawaiian. Listen!"

Jazz coughs, as though smothering a giggle, and crosses her eyes at me from her perch behind Macie. As if in great concentration, Macie squares her shoulders and twists up her face. "May-lay Kali-ke-mock-a." Her voice grows louder as she sounds out the Hawaiian phrase, a cocky smile plumping her already chubby cheeks.

"Good job, squirt." I cross my eyes at Jazz.

She giggle-coughs again, then motions to the bag in my hands. "Good shopping trip?"

"I guess." I cross into the kitchen and put away

the groceries before rejoining Jazz and Macie in the living room. "Thanks for hanging out with Macie while we were gone."

"No problem." Jazz flashes that famous Cheshire-cat grin of hers, but something more solemn flickers behind her silvery gaze.

"Macie?" I tug on one of my sister's curls. "Why don't you go see if Gramma needs help making dinner."

Macie's eyes grow wide at the magic word—dinner—and she scampers into the kitchen without a second glance. "Is everything okay?" I keep my voice soft, so Macie's snoopy little ears can't pick up on anything they shouldn't.

"Yeah." Jazz shrugs. "I'm great." A bob of her head.

"*Really.*" I raise my brows.

"Well..." She dips her head and picks at the liner of her prosthetic leg.

I knew it. I grab Jazz's hand and give it a tug. "Let's go out front."

She clambers to her feet, wobbling a little as she does so, and follows me down the hall to the front porch. We settle onto the swing and, after checking to make sure the window is shut, I turn to Jazz. "Come on. Spill."

Jazz nibbles her lip. "It's really nothing. I shouldn't get into it. Ruby will be here to pick me up soon."

I roll my eyes at her. "You think you can pull that with me? No way. Your aunt can wait in the car if she has to."

"Fine." A sigh. "Mom's in rehab."

"*What?*" A jolt of electricity shoots through me, and I take a moment to study Jazz. "Wait. Isn't that a good thing?"

Something—a tear?—shimmers in the corner of Jazz's eye, and she stares past me to the waves crashing on the beach across the street. "I guess it's a good thing. But..." she shakes her head. "It's dumb."

I open my mouth to offer words of comfort, but I can't think of any that would help. Instead, I scooch closer to Jazz on the swing. Tension rolls from her in waves as we sit in the warm, decidedly un-Christmassy sunshine.

Finally, Jazz turns to face me again. "Mom always tried to sober up for Christmas. Most years she'd even go to church with me for the candlelight service. But this year…" Jazz shakes her head. "I won't even get to see her."

"Because she's in rehab." A cold lump mushrooms in my stomach. Christmas is going to be hard enough knowing that my own mom is dead, but what must it be like for Jazz—knowing that her mom is very much alive, but holed up in a rehab center somewhere?

"Maybe you could visit her."

"I don't even know if I want to." Jazz adjusts her position on the swing, thunking her prosthesis against the ground. "It's…weird. And hard."

"Tell me about it." I rest my chin in my hands and stare out at the neighbor islands, Lanai and Molokai, across the channel. "Gramma was telling me today about how Mom always used to send her a Christmas stocking every year. But now she won't have one. None of us will—or, if we do, it won't be the same."

"I don't care about the presents. We never did stockings or stuff like that." Jazz tugs on her long, sandy-colored braid. "I'll just miss…*her*. We've never been close, but family is family. You know?"

"Right." That lump in my stomach hardens into a hockey puck. *God, help me quit being so selfish.* I sit in the quiet for a few minutes before something Jazz said starts niggling at my brain. "Wait. You mean you've never gotten a Christmas stocking? Like, candy and Chapstick and jewelry and stuff like that?"

Jazz shakes her head. "A few times when I was little, Mom would take me to Whaler's General on Christmas Eve and let me pick out a stuffed animal or something, but then she started spending more money on booze than Christmas presents."

I'm hit with a stab of pain for my friend, but Jazz only smiles, like she *didn't* have the most horrendous childhood I could imagine.

"My favorite part of the holiday was always going to church on Christmas eve." A wicked gleam flickers in Jazz's eyes. "At least there I always got a candy cane." She says it like she's expecting me to laugh, so I do, even though my soul is crying for this incredible girl who's been given so much less than she deserves.

Words tumble around in my mouth, sidestepping my tongue and refusing to stay in place long enough for me to string any of them together into an appropriate response. Before I can force the words to cooperate, a growling sound echoes from farther down the street, announcing Jazz's Aunt Ruby—or, more accurately, her dinged-up minivan.

"Guess I'd better go." Jazz stands and heads for

the front steps as Ruby's car pulls alongside the curb, engine sputtering. "See ya." She waves her fist in a *shaka,* thumb and pinky extended.

I return the gesture and smile before heading in for dinner, but that hockey puck in my stomach keeps me from eating more than a few bites of Thanksgiving leftovers.

"Isn't it funny how quickly a person can get tired of turkey?" Gramma glances at my nearly full plate and *tsks.* "Olive, would you like something else? I could get you a couple slices of bread to turn that into a sandwich."

I shake my head. "Sorry, Grams. I'm not hungry tonight." How can I be, when all I can think about is a Macie-sized version of Jazz waking up every Christmas morning to an empty stocking? Did she even *hang* a stocking?

I pick up my fork and drag it through a pile of lukewarm mashed potatoes, but I can't make myself take a bite.

If anything on this earth was half as bad as celebrating Christmas without family, it would be celebrating without presents.

And, after all that Jazz has been through, she shouldn't have to encounter any more sadness this year. Especially not at Christmas.

Chapter Two

"WANNA GRAB A SHAVE ICE?"

"Brander, hey!" The voice on the other end of the line—the same one that's been blaring out of every Hawaiian radio for the last few months—brings a smile to my face that comes through in my voice. "I'd love to. But...are you sure you have time?"

"I'll make time." My worship-leader-turned-superstar friend laughs. "Want me to pick you up?"

"That'd be great."

I smile again as we hang up, then run to the upstairs bathroom I share with Macie to freshen up. I'm still in the dress I wore to church earlier this morning, but my caramel-colored tumbleweed of hair could use some attention. A splash of lip gloss wouldn't hurt either.

Not that this is a date or anything, but still—it never hurts to put on a little makeup. Especially when you're hanging out with a pseudo-celebrity.

But when I answer Brander's knock on the door fifteen minutes later, any thoughts of celebrities—or dating, for that matter—fly from my brain. Because the Brander standing before me, with his lean, toned forearms and jaunty ebony cowlick, isn't the pop star that the kids at youth group gossip about. He's just...*Brander.*

And, no matter what ever happens between us, I know I'll always be thankful that he came into my life when he did.

"How's your weekend been?" he asks once we're zipping down the road in his fireball-red Porsche.

"Okay, I guess." I raise my hands. "Weird."

He nods and we fall silent, the wind whistling in my ears for a while before he turns onto Front Street and opens his mouth. "Sounds like things have been pretty rough for Jazz too."

"About her mom, you mean?"

"Yeah."

The rumble of the Porsche's motor echoes in the air for a second before the words burst out of my mouth. "Did you know Jazz's never had a real Christmas before? Like, no presents or stocking or anything? Because I know Christmas isn't supposed to be all about presents and stuff, but still. That's not fair."

"Are you suggesting something?" Brander's words are a challenge.

"What do you mean?"

"I mean, what are we going to do to make things better for her?" Brander pulls into a parking spot across from the Shave Ice Shack and hops out.

"You mean like a secret Santa kind of thing?" My mind takes off on a road trip down memory lane to the good old days—back when I was little, and Mom laid a chocolate snowman or other Christmassy surprise on my pillow every night during the Advent season. Sometimes there was a note too, signed, "The Head Elf."

Brander bobs his head and motions me toward the line winding away from the Shave Ice Shack. "Remember what they talked about at the support group?"

"Huh? They talked about a *lot* at support group. And I heard way more than you did—you know, since I didn't go running off to become a celebrity." I soften the words with a wink and a soft jab to his elbow, but Brander flinches anyway.

"Don't remind me. I hate backing out on stuff."

"I didn't mean it like that." I shake my head and swallow a laugh. For someone so laid-back, Brander sure does take his commitments seriously. *Too* seriously, sometimes. "Recording a single in Nashville is a whole lot more important than volunteering at Jonah's support group."

Brander shrugs. "Depends on how you see it."

"Anyway." I shift my feet, sand slipping inside my flip-flops—*slippas*, as the locals call them—and scraping between my toes. "What were you going to say?"

Brander blows out a long, steady stream of air. One of those voice-control exercises he always talks about? "Nothing really. Just that I remember one day Jonah talked about how sometimes helping cheer someone else up is the best way to make *yourself* feel better. Maybe we could do something to help Jazz get in the Christmas spirit—and maybe it would help you too."

Something within me shimmies, almost like my heart is ringing a cluster of jingle bells. "That would be really cool. But what could we do?"

"What *couldn't* we do?" Brander grins and plops a pair of koa-wood sunglasses onto his nose, hiding his chocolate-covered-almond eyes.

A tremor of anticipation flies through me as we make our way to the front of the line and order our shave ices. As soon as we've started toward the beach, I turn to Brander. "Tell me what you're thinking. About Jazz."

He scoops a spoonful of *lilikoi*—passionfruit—shave ice into his mouth before answering. "I don't know. But my parents have done stuff like this before—picked one of their employees during the holidays and blessed their socks off."

"Maybe..." I take a bite of my own shave ice, letting the sweet, powdery crystals dissolve on my tongue—the closest I'll get to snow this year. "Maybe we could make her a stocking. Like my mom used to do for the rest of the family."

"Just a stocking?" Brander raises an eyebrow and plops onto a bench before motioning for me to join him.

"Not *just* a stocking." I sink onto the weathered wood, my elbow bumping Brander's as I lean back. "She used to go all out—there'd be more stuff in the stocking than there was under the tree. We could make Jazz some crazy kind of secret-Santa stocking, then give it to her on—wait." I squint at Brander in the vibrant sunlight. "Are you even going to be here for Christmas? Don't they want you out on tour to promote your single or something?"

"Not sure." Brander digs in the bottom of his cone and comes back with a spoonful of ice cream. "I know Mike was talking to a few people, but nothing ever got decided by the time I flew back for Thanksgiving. I guess we'll have to wait and see."

"Right." I purse my lips. Can't the Christian music industry survive without Brander until the New Year? It wasn't like they hadn't been living without him for the last few decades. "Then I guess we'd better get started now."

Brander nods.

We eat in silence for a moment before my hand strays to my pocket. "Would you mind...I think it might really lift Grams' spirits if she could help too. She's been pretty down this weekend, and I know how close she and Jazz are."

"Sure." Brander tips back his cone to drink the melted remains of his shave ice.

Not bothering to finish my own, I set it on the bench before standing and taking a few steps toward the waves. I pull out my phone and scroll down to tap Gramma's number. The rings echo in my ear—one...two—

"Mele Kalikimaka!" A decidedly *non*-Grandma-like voice giggles on the other line. "That means Merry Christmas."

"Yeah, I know squirt. Where's Gramma?"

"She's right here." Gramma's warm timbre fills

my ear—she must have picked up the other extension of her ancient landline. "What's up?"

I quickly explain the plan. "I thought you might want to help out."

"I do! I do!" Macie squeaks on the other line. "Can we put a puppy in her stocking?"

"A puppy?" A chill runs down my spine, despite the fact that I'm no longer as terrified of dogs as I was at the beginning of the year. "Maybe a stuffed one."

"Oh." I can almost see Macie's bottom lip pooching out.

"What about you, Grams?"

"I like it. Christmas is the perfect time to bless others. Why don't I take Macie down for a shave ice? That way we can all do some brainstorming."

"Sounds good." I force an extra note of brightness into my voice—Macie was *not* part of the original plan.

Then again, how much trouble can a mermaid-obsessed six-year-old really cause?

Chapter Three

I SHOULD'VE KNOWN BETTER. WE HAVEN'T even made it through the checkout line at one of the many jewelry stores on Front Street, and Macie's already managed to spill half of her shave ice on a sales clerk, stomp on a stray cat's tail—accidentally, of course—and send one of those dashboard hula-girls toppling to her untimely death.

I groan under my breath and lean close to whisper in Brander's ear. "Not what I had in mind."

"What do you mean? Jazz'll love the anklet."

"That might be true." In fact, knowing Jazz and her sense of humor, she'll probably end up fastening it around her prosthetic leg. A smile tugs at the corner of my mouth. "But Macie must be driving you bonkers."

"No way." Brander shakes his head, his glossy ebony cowlick flopping over the crown of his head. "Life as an only child can get boring. Your sister is—"

"*Not* boring." I roll my eyes and hurry over to keep Macie from slipping a tropical-themed charm bracelet onto her wrist.

By the time we've maneuvered our way back onto the traffic jam of humanity that is Hawaii's favorite shopping street, I'm beat and my wallet is several bills lighter. Maybe this is going to be harder than I'd thought.

Thankfully at the next store we stop in, Brander flashes me a thumbs-up over Macie's head before grabbing her hand and steering her toward a table overflowing with free cookie samples.

"I used to get these for the kids in my Sunday school class." Gramma hands me a box of pineapple-shaped cookies. "Jazz always seemed to be especially fond of the chocolate-chip macadamia ones."

A pang echoes in my stomach at Gramma's words, and a memory creeps to the forefront of my brain. "Mom used to make chocolate-macadamia-nut shortbread every year for our church's cookie exchange party." The words slip past my tongue before I can stop them, and I hang my head. Leave it to me to cast a pall over the afternoon.

But when I chance a peek at Gramma, she's *almost* smiling. "She got that from me. I always make macadamia nut shortbread for Christmas, though she must have added the chocolate herself."

"Really?"

Grams nods, and a little warm glow lights in my chest as we step up to the checkout counter. Somehow the simple knowledge that Mom's special tradition was Gramma's to begin with is that much more comforting to me. It's almost like...

She's right here with us.

Today, tomorrow, and maybe even the next day—all the way through this entire holiday season.

And knowing that makes everything shine a little bit brighter.

Chapter Four

"Guess what we did in art class today!" Macie bursts through the front door after school the following week, her backpack spilling half-completed worksheets across the entryway.

"What?" I cast a sideways glance at Gramma, who is busy lining the front window with multicolor twinkle lights. We won't put up our tree—fake, unfortunately—until the weekend, but Gramma seems determined to make the place as festive as possible until then.

"Teacher had us each count out twenty-five strips of paper and then we stapled them together and made this chain—" Macie slides her backpack from her shoulders and digs around in it before coming up with a haphazard red-and-green paper chain. "And we get to take off one link every day before Christmas."

"Oh." My gaze runs from Macie's hand to the end of the chain. That's it—only twenty-five short days until Christmas. We don't even have a tree—and

Jazz's Christmas stocking is nothing more than an odd jumble of cookies, jewelry, and random knick-knacks. A long, miserable monologue bubbles up in my throat, but I swallow it back and smile down at Macie. "It's great."

"Thanks." Her cheeks plump in a smile and she turns to Gramma. "I'm gonna go hang it up in my room."

"Whoa, now. We don't need any more junk cluttering up *our* room." I clear my throat.

"Junk?" Macie's lip quivers, and the smile fades from her face. A tear wells in the corner of her eye, and she sniffs. "I thought you said it was pretty."

"Well, yeah." My stomach snarls in an ugly knot. When will my tongue learn to edit itself? "But I don't think it's the right fit for our room. It should be somewhere else. Somewhere it can be appreciated. Like the dining room." My gaze darts over to Gramma, but she's too tangled up with that string of lights to offer any support.

Macie casts me a wary glance, then drops the chain and gives it a kick with her bare foot, toes curled. "No. You're right. It's dumb and crooked and ugly."

"Hey, I didn't say that." The knot of guilt grows

bigger. "I think it's cute." As cute as construction paper and staples can be, at least.

Clearly not convinced of my sudden affinity for the chain, Macie wipes a tear from her eye. And another. Something that sounds suspiciously like the start of a wail squeaks in her throat, and she blinks down at the chain. "All I wanted was to do something special for Christmas—like *Mommy* used to."

"Aw, Macie. You know it's not *your* job to make Christmas special, right? Jesus already did that. I know things are tough this year, but everything's going to be okay. Promise." I bend down until I'm eye level with her and open my arms to invite a hug, but Macie brushes past me and stomps across the living room.

"Nothing is gonna be okay." She flops onto the couch and buries her curly head in a pillow. "Mommy's not here so we're not going to make our special Christmassy cookies, and Santa Claus is a big lie. Just like the kids at school said."

"Whoa there. What's all this about Santa Claus?" Gramma finally strings up the last of the lights, then crosses to the couch and smooths Macie's tangled mop of hair.

"Kanani told me yesterday that Santa isn't real."

Macie lifts her head and sniffs. "So I prayed last night that, if Santa *was* real, he'd send one of the elves to tell me so. N-no one came."

I stand to the side, hands in my Harvard University sweatshirt pocket, until Gramma catches my eye and motions me forward. *Say something*, her gaze seems to beg, so I open my mouth and let the first thing I can think of spill out. "Of course Santa didn't send one of his elves to Hawaii, silly. Santa still thinks you live in Boston. In fact, I bet the elf gave Daddy a message for you."

"You really think so?" Macie gapes up at me, eyes wide.

"Of course." I scuff my foot against the floor. I'd better fill Dad in on all this before Macie can get to Gramma's phone and call him to double-check my story.

"Now, what else did you say? Something about Christmas cookies?" Gramma tugs on one of Macie's curls, and my little sister finally cracks a smile.

"We haven't made any yet. I want Mommy's special chocolate-macadamia ones."

"I think that can be arranged." A smile sneaks onto Gramma's face, and she stands and heads to the kitchen. "Olive? Macie? Ready for kitchen elf duty?"

Macie jumps from the couch and runs to the kitchen so fast she practically leaves a trail of dust behind her. My stomach growls at the thought of a freshly baked shortbread cookie, but I know I'd better give Dad a call first.

Raising a finger, I dodge into the hallway and dig out my phone. He doesn't answer, so I leave a quick message before rejoining the others in the kitchen.

One hour and half a dozen tastes of cookie dough later, we're all huddled around a pan of fresh-out-of-the-oven shortbread, the nutty, buttery smell curling up and wafting into my nose.

I lick my lips and pretend I don't notice when Macie shoves an entire cookie into her mouth at once. In fact, I'm about to do the same when Gramma's ancient landline lets out a piercing ring.

"Daddy! I'll get it!" Macie grabs another cookie on her way to the phone, and I roll my eyes at Gramma.

Sure enough, it is Dad on the phone. He must have listened to my message, because Macie's eyes grow wider and wider before she bursts out with a long string of questions about elves and reindeer and who-knows-what-else.

I lean back against the counter and listen until Gramma whispers in my ear. "Come with me."

I trail after her, Macie's excited chit-chat following us until we're standing in front of the upstairs storage room.

"Is everything okay?" I peer at Gramma. The last time Gramma and I were alone up here was right before Jazz told me she had cancer.

"Oh, yes. Fine." Gramma's eyes crinkle, and she pats my back. "I want to show you something. Now, before we get swept up in the craziness of the holidays." She lifts a hand and turns the doorknob before stepping inside.

I follow, flipping the light switch to illuminate the musty oversized storage closet, but Gramma seems to know exactly where she's going even without a light. She's already digging through a crumbling old cardboard container by the time the old overhead light finally flickers to life.

"Do you remember this?" Gramma straightens and hands me a clear glass ball filled with tiny, shimmery snowflakes and a blown-glass Christmas present. Something stirs faintly in my heart, but I shake my head.

"Should I?"

"I suppose not. You were awfully young at the time." She lifts the ornament so it catches the light, illuminating the crystalline snow trapped inside the ball.

"Was it mine?"

Gramma purses her lips and gazes at the delicate glass globe for a moment before handing it to me. I take it and cradle it between my fingers as though I'm holding a handful of dandelion fluff.

"This was in my Christmas stocking one year, from your mother. She said that you and she picked it out together. For me." Her voice catches, but both of her eyes are dry. "It's been my favorite ornament ever since."

"*Oh.*" I grip it a little bit tighter, my heart pinching in my chest. There are moments with my mom that I can't remember. That I've forgotten about. *How could I?* My hand trembles.

"How—how old was I?" I cringe as my own voice cracks over the words.

"Three. Maybe four." Gramma shakes her head. "Like I said, too young to remember."

"Thanks for showing me anyway." I drink in the sight of the ornament for one long second before handing the ball back to Grams. Once again, a strange flicker of recognition pangs in my chest, but the memory is too hazy, too far away to retrieve.

And so, with a heart that is void of memories and burdened with grief, I follow Gramma out of the closet, down the stairs, and back into this new, unfamiliar life I'm learning to call my own.

Chapter Five

BELLY WARMED BY A STEAMING MUG of hot cocoa, I perch next to Jazz as Gramma wobbles on a stepstool and fastens a glittery star to the top of the tree. The fake tree.

"We always got a real one in Boston." I lower my voice and lean close to Jazz so Gramma won't hear me complain. "It made the whole house smell like an evergreen forest all through December."

Jazz lowers her mug and licks whipped cream from her upper lip. "I've never had a Christmas tree before. There was no room on the boat, and Aunt Ruby isn't the festive type."

My heart twinges, and I take another sip of cocoa. "That stinks."

"It was tough when I was little. Now I'm kind of glad—I grew up learning about the real Christmas, instead of all the Santa stuff."

I nod. "That's good, I guess." Still, it must have made for a pretty dreary holiday.

"Not that there's anything wrong with Santa or

anything like that.”

“I know.” My gaze wanders over to Macie, who is so excited about Santa and elves and everything else that has to do with Christmas that she’s spinning across the living room like a runaway top. “Still. Maybe Macie should learn more about the real Christmas.”

“Maybe.” Jazz bobs her shoulders and sets her cocoa mug on the coffee table before clambering to her feet. Her prosthesis clunks against the floor as she steps over to the tree, but her stride is smoother. Steadier. She’s healing—am I?

“Jingle, jingle, jingle *bells!*” Macie creates her own harmonies to sing along with Gramma’s Sinatra CD, shaking her hands and shimmying her hips in what I’m pretty sure is some sort of an attempt at the hula. Or maybe she’s trying to dance like a Rockette. Either way, she keeps rocking all around the Christmas tree as Gramma and Jazz hang the first ornaments.

“Come on, Olive. Lend a hand.” Jazz grins at me as she fastens a shining silver starfish to one of the tree’s highest boughs. “This is really fun.”

“You go ahead.” I take another sip of cocoa and burrow back deeper into the armchair. “It’s just as much fun watching.”

Watching.

I've been doing a lot of watching this year. Too much, probably.

Gramma's old-school CD turntable clacks and clunks, and another song starts playing, this one straight from some of my earliest childhood memories.

O little town of Bethlehem, how still we see thee lie,

Above thy deep and dreamless sleep the silent stars go by.

And then, right as Gramma lifts Mom's ornament, the one she showed me earlier this week, out of a box, I remember.

"Grams, wait." I spring from my seat. "I just want to—can I hold it again? Just for a second?"

The serene, soft smile Gramma offers me says more than her words ever could. She crosses the room and hands over the ornament with a knowing nod, then bends and procures another bauble from the box. "Take your time, sweetie. Hang it wherever you'd like when you're done."

I nod, too many words clogged in my throat for an answer to slip out, and trace the spirals carved in the surface of the glass ball. A feathery wisp of a memory sends shivers all the way down to my toes, and tears spring to my eyes as the old, familiar carol continues to pour from Gramma's chintzy speakers.

Yet in thy dark streets shineth the everlasting Light;

The hopes and fears of all the years are met in thee tonight.

I sway back and forth in time to the music, eyes fixed on the ornament. Maybe I don't remember *it* so much as I do the day Mom and I bought it. Even that memory is hazy—wrapping-paper thin—but it's there. It's as though I can still hear the jingle of bells on the door of one of Mom's favorite purveyors of knick-knacks. Smell the cinnamon-sugar air. Feel Mom's mittened hand clasped tightly around my own. Squeezing once. Twice. Three times.

"You okay?" Jazz's voice comes from a startlingly close distance, and I nearly jump.

"Fine. I'll be even better if you don't sneak up on me like that." I wink to soften my words, then hold up the ornament. "Just getting all sappy and sentimental. Sorry."

"Sorry?" Jazz waves a hand in the air. "Don't be. Sappy and sentimental is what Christmas is all about."

I smile at her, then hold the ornament up to eye level. "Mom and I bought this ornament for Grams when I was really little, but I don't remember it too well."

Jazz opens her mouth, but before she can respond, Macie careens around the couch, belting at the top of her tiny lungs about "Rudolph the Red-Nosed Reindeer." Eyes shut tight, my sister leaps into the air and lands only inches from my feet. Not bothering to open her eyes, she spins in a circle, then jumps again—in my direction

Her soft, fluffy tummy knocks against me as she lands, and my knees buckle. Macie's eyes finally open as the ornament—the precious link to Mom I've been holding so gently—flies out of my hand and shoots up, up, up...and into the air.

Despite the Hawaiian-style holiday heat and humidity, every vein in my body freezes over as the ornament begins its slow, graceful collision course with the floor.

A strangled yelp escapes from my throat as Jazz and I both reach for the precious glass ball, but it's too late. Macie dodges the flying orb seconds before it meets the floor and explodes into a million minuscule shards of glass. The snowflakes inside leap into the air in a puff, then settle on the floor around the broken pieces. The present that, just moments ago, had dangled merrily inside the ball, lies in the middle of the mess, a chip in its curled glass ribbon.

"What was that?" Gramma turns from fastening a string of seashells to a low-hanging branch. Her gaze sweeps the room before coming to land on the disaster area beneath my feet. Her eyes grow wide, and the usual rosiness fades from her cheeks. "Oh...*my*."

Macie surveys the mess before sticking her thumb in her mouth. "Whoops." It comes out in a small, sad voice—one that says she already knows she's in Big Trouble.

Jazz's brow crumples, and she steps away from the mess. "I'll get the vacuum," she murmurs before disappearing down the hall.

I stand, heart crunching in my chest, tears brimming in my eyes, a thousand words quivering in my throat. Words of fury, sadness, and confusion. Right when I'd started to remember, the ornament— the memory—is gone. Forever.

And so is Mom.

Tears send the floor shaking and quivering beneath my gaze, but that doesn't stop me from swooping down and grabbing the present before Jazz can reappear with the vacuum.

The jagged part of the ribbon digs into my palm, but I hold on.

Tight.

"I'm sorry I made Olive drop the ball, Grammy," Macie says for the hundredth time that night, over a rather solemn dinner of soggy Spam musubi.

"It's okay, sweetie." Gramma reaches over and squeezes Macie's hand. The light in her eyes is dim, and a half-smile slides off her face as she glances at the tree. Somehow it doesn't seem near as pretty without Mom's ornament. "I know it wasn't on purpose."

Macie shrugs and picks at her Spam—a true indication of how much this has shaken her. "If it was okay, Olive wouldn't be mad at me."

"Who said I was mad?" I cross my arms and push away my plate. No chance I'm getting any more of that mystery meat past the lump in my throat.

"You look mad." Macie narrows her gaze at me

from across the table and tightens her fist around her fork. "Are *you* mad, Jazzie?"

"Of course not, squirt." Jazz reaches over to pinch Macie's chubby forearm. "We all make mistakes," she adds, nodding at me with a sage expression.

"I guess." I duck my head and pat my sweater pocket. I don't know what made me snatch the present, and I'm even more unsure why I didn't hand it over to Gramma, but I know I'm going to hang onto it. Tight.

Something pinches in my chest, and I lift my gaze to find Macie staring at me, eyes wide and gaze hollow. "Do you forgive me, Olive?"

"Sure I do." I force one corner of my mouth up into what could almost be called a smile, then take one more bite of rice. It goes down a little easier this time. "After all, Christmas isn't about *stuff* anyway. At least, that's what Jazz says."

Jazz nods, her braid flopping over one shoulder. "It sounds cheesy, but it's true." She shrugs, and something in her eyes adds *I learned that the hard way.*

But even if Jazz really believes that—even if *I* believe it—that doesn't make things a whole lot better. The evening stretches on, and the glass present stashed in my sweater seems to weigh down not only my pocket but also my heart.

But the heaviness inside doesn't leave when I hang my sweater up before bed—in fact, it only seems to grow. Night falls, draping its shadows around the corners of the bedroom like a knitted afghan, and Macie seems to have little trouble slipping off to a dream-world of dancing sugarplums. But though my eyelids grow heavy and my vision blurs, I don't drift off to sleep

The sound of ocean waves grows fuzzy as a warm breeze brushes across my cheeks, and that's when it comes—a soft noise. A gentle whisper.

"Christmas wasn't created for us to spend the month of December focusing on making *ourselves* happy. Christmas is about giving—of our time, our money, and our hearts. Christmas isn't about material things. It's about *love*."

If anyone else had dared tell me that tonight, I probably wouldn't have given the words a second thought, but since the words in my head sound suspiciously like something Mom would've told me when I was little, I don't fight them.

In fact, as I nestle down into my covers and hug a pillow against my chest, I let them loop through my mind again. And again.

One last time.

A polar chill runs through me, despite the sticky, warm Tradewinds blowing through the open window.

All that stuff Mom used to say every year—about giving and not receiving, about being lights in the darkest part of the year—maybe it means more than I ever gave her credit for.

Maybe it means that a shattered ornament really isn't that big of a deal. Maybe it means that I should spend less time wallowing and more time focusing on what I can do to help Macie and Grams have the best Christmas ever. On what I can do to brighten Jazz's holiday—on what I can do to help one very, very special friend.

Chapter Six

"You're still upset about that ornament, aren't you?" Jazz purses her lips and gives me her famous silver-eyed stare after church the next morning.

"Wouldn't you be? It was another link to my mom—and now it's gone."

"At least you had a link to begin with." Jazz lowers her eyes. "I called the rehab place to talk to Mom last night, but they said she was in a group session. It was almost nine o'clock. I don't think they do sessions that late. I'm betting she told them to tell me that. Just because she didn't feel like talking to me."

"Ouch." If I were Jazz, I would've lost hope long ago. "But you still miss her, huh?"

"Like you wouldn't believe." Jazz's gaze drifts to the clouds hovering above the West Maui Mountains. "I know she and I didn't have the usual relationship and all that, but still—she's my mom. This'll be the first Christmas we aren't together."

I sigh and bow my head, the ocean waves beyond the church pavilion crashing in my ears. *God, can't*

You do something? People always say that Christmas is the season of miracles.

*Then again…*a fresh breeze blows my hair away from my face as something stirs in my chest. I shouldn't put so much pressure on God. Maybe sometimes it's up to *me* to make things brighter. For all of us.

"Hey." I yank on Jazz's braid. "Want to go Christmas shopping?"

"For what?"

"Christmas stuff." I laugh and give her braid another tug. "I'm going to try and find a new ornament for Grams—it won't be the same as the one I dropped, but I want to make it up to her somehow." Besides, if I bring Jazz shopping with me, there's a chance she'll point out stuff I can sneak back and buy for her stocking later.

The Whaler's Village shopping center isn't too far away from Lahaina, but it's worlds away in terms of class and style. Instead of Front Street's eclectic mix of designer boutiques and kooky tourist traps,

Whaler's Village offers a manicured, open-air square filled with high-end storefronts and eateries.

"I guess we should have stayed in town." I bite my lip and picture the meager contents of my wallet. It won't stretch very far here, if first impressions are anything to go by. Gramma'd better let me start working at the Shave Ice Shack again after the new year, because I'm already almost flat broke.

"Oh, well." Jazz shrugs and points to an elevator. "Let's go up and get something to eat."

I follow her lead, and after a quick lunch of bahn mi burgers—a first for me, but definitely not a last— we backtrack to the first floor to begin our browsing. Jazz wanders all over the place. Even with her prosthesis, I can barely keep up as she pops from store to store.

Everywhere we go, I comb the aisles for an ornament that might remind Gramma of the one she lost, but there's nothing.

"What about this?" Jazz lifts a google-eyed starfish ornament and snickers.

"Yeah, no." I roll my eyes and laugh, but inside I'm groaning. Why couldn't I have kept a tighter hold on that ornament when Macie decided to bowl me over?

"Don't give up." Jazz squeezes my arm as we take

the elevator back up to the second floor. "Besides— the holidays aren't *really* about fancy ornaments and stuff. Remember?"

"That's what *somebody* keeps telling me, anyway." I close my eyes so Jazz won't see them rolling around in my head. "But everyone knows that those things make the season a whole lot more exciting."

"Maybe for some people." The elevator doors whoosh open, and Jazz bites her lip as we step outside.

I sigh and trudge after Jazz, her words playing on a continuous loop as we walk through store after store. Maybe Jazz is so into this reason-for-the-season business because she's never known any different. She's never had a chance to experience the joy of a fun-filled Christmas for herself.

That's why it's my job to do everything I can to make this year extra-special. Just for her.

We enter an indie gift boutique, and I keep one eye trained on Jazz as she drifts over to admire a stack of hand-lettered quotes.

She runs a hand over several of them before letting out a snicker. "I should totally get this for Aunt Ruby." She laughs again, then hands me the quote.

"'Today's menu—eat it or starve.'" I bite back a grin. "Is Ruby a kitchen whiz?"

"She's the *worst*. Last night I caught her trying to bake gingersnaps. Without the *snap*." She shudders for good measure. "They were like packed sand. *Burnt* packed sand."

I make a face, and we keep browsing. By the time we're done, I've got a few more ideas for trinkets to stuff in Jazz's stocking, and Jazz is the proud owner of a certain quote for a certain chef.

"I can't believe you're really going to give it to her." I snort.

"She'll love it." Jazz peeks inside her bag. "She's got a good sense of—hey, Brander."

I lift my head and a smile blooms on my face as Brander bounds around a corner. He raises his hand in a *shaka,* and Jazz and I return the gesture.

"Christmas shopping?" Jazz lifts a brow.

Brander nods. "You too?"

"Trying to find something for my gramma." I launch into a brief explanation of yesterday's ornament disaster.

"Ouch." Brander flinches when I'm done. "That stinks. But you shouldn't feel like you have to make it up to her or replace the ornament. Sometimes we place too much importance on tangible objects, when they're really only the wrappings of a memory."

"You sound just like Jazz." I bump his shoulder with my own, then smile at Jazz. "Not that that's a bad thing, of course."

Brander opens his mouth as if to say more, but his phone cuts him off with an obnoxious buzz. He pulls it out and switches off the ringer before glancing down at the screen and grimacing. "Rats. It's Mike."

"Record label Mike?" Jazz's eyes open wide, and Brander nods.

"That is too cool," Jazz says to me as Brander answers the phone and takes a few steps away. "I forget that Brander's, like, famous now."

"But...I mean, he's still—you know. *Brander.*" My stomach clenches at the thought of him hanging out with a crowd of celebrities on the mainland. That seems so unlike the guy I met earlier in the year—the island boy with a koa wood guitar and huge heart for Jesus.

"Brander can be Brander and still be famous." Jazz grins. "I think it's the coolest. Imagine the first time he wins a Grammy—we can say we knew him when."

"I'd rather still know him." I shove my hands in

my pockets and stare down at a river of moss running between two cobblestones.

"Sorry about that." Brander's Oxford-clad feet appear at the top of my line of sight. "Mike's in a frenzy, and I can't get a good signal here. Catch you later?"

I look up in time to see the wrinkle of Brander's forehead, the fading light in his eyes as he pockets his phone and pulls out his car keys.

"No problem. Go do all your rock star business." Jazz tosses him a grin that I struggle to replicate, and Brander dashes off with a wave and a "goodbye" thrown over his shoulder.

"What do you think is going on?" I stare after him as he sprints around a corner.

"Who knows? Maybe they finally worked it out so he can go on tour over the holidays."

"Maybe." I adjust my purse. "You want to go anywhere else?"

"Nah." Jazz shakes her head, so we start toward the bus stop. Though there's a spring in her step, I can't summon the same kind of enthusiasm.

If Brander leaves on tour, that'll be one more person missing this Christmas.

And even though he might not be family, Brander is definitely part of my heart's *ohana*.

Later that afternoon I'm sitting on the couch, bookended by Gramma and Macie, watching a glitter-and-glam Hollywood Christmas spectacular when my phone dings with a text.

Brander?

Gramma gives me the stink eye as I reach into my pocket, but I pretend not to notice as I pull out my phone and scroll through my notifications. Not Brander. Dad.

There's an early Christmas present waiting for you and Macie out front. Make sure to take it inside before you girls go to bed.

A Christmas present, huh? From the dad who forgot to call and wish us a happy Thanksgiving? I pinch my lips against a scoff and relay the message to Macie, who immediately bounces up from the couch and races to the front hall. Chancing a backward glance at Gramma, I catch a twinkle in her eye as I trail after my sister.

Macie barely waits for me to step into the entryway before she swings the front door open wide. For a second, I can't see anything in the dusky evening light, but as my eyes adjust, I catch sight of a man's white beard. And—is that—

"Ho, ho, ho! Merry Christmas." The voice is strong and warm, but it's far too young to belong to Santa Claus.

Especially since I know that voice—know exactly who it belongs to.

Chapter Seven

"DADDY!" MACIE HURLS HERSELF AT DAD, and he staggers back at the impact.

"Whoa, munchkin. You've done some growing since September." He laughs and rights himself, then steps across the threshold and pulls off a chintzy fake Santa beard, revealing a jolly smile that I haven't seen in nearly a year.

I stand, mouth open, as he hangs it on Gramma's purse hook. Dad catches my eye and laughs. "Guess it was pretty silly of me to wear a Santa suit in Maui." He takes off his Santa jacket and matching hat, then wipes a bead of sweat from his forehead. "How are you?"

"We're amazing. Fantastic! Splendiferous! Especially now that you're here." Macie hops up and down and throws herself into Dad's arms once again.

He chuckles and strokes her mane of unruly curls, then releases her and takes a step toward me. "Olive?"

"I think she's speechless, Alex." Gramma pads over to lean against the doorframe.

"I'm not speechless." I swallow against the lump in my throat that seems to be keeping any more words from coming out. "I'm just...wow. This is a surprise."

Dad's smile fades, and he throws his arm around me in a quick side-hug. He backs off before I can react, even though I don't know what I would've done if I'd had the time. Part of me is dying to fall into Dad's arms and hug him tight. The other part of me wants to examine him like he's some sort of foreign species of fish washed ashore after a big storm.

I cross my arms, as if that can help keep my emotions tucked neatly inside my heart. "What are you doing here?"

Dad's eyes cloud over, and I dig my fingers into my palm. Maybe I should have gone for the hug-and-cry kind of welcome, after all.

Thankfully the look in Dad's eyes clears with a single blink, and he grins at me and Macie. "I came to bring Christmas, of course." He ducks back outside and reappears with a stack of presents. "Is there room for these under the tree?"

"Absolutely." Macie nods faster than a bobblehead. "Are they for *me*?"

"And for Olive and your grandmother." Dad walks into the living room, not bothering to remove his goofy patent-leather Santa boots. I cringe as they leave thick black scuff marks on the polished floor. No doubt Gramma will have her mop out the second Dad turns in for the night.

"You're right on time, Alex. Meatloaf's about done." Gramma doesn't bat an eye at Dad's boot-clad feet as she bustles over to the kitchen and slips on her trademark plumeria-print apron.

"You were in on this too?" I whirl around and gawk at Gramma.

"I didn't think anything could make Christmas merrier than a visit from Santa himself." Grams winks at me, then motions to a pot on the stove. "Mash the potatoes for me, Olive?"

I nod and get to work, but I keep an ear tuned to Macie and Dad's conversation.

"How long are you staying? Will you go to church with us on Christmas Eve?"

"Of course I'll come to church. And my flight doesn't leave until New Year's Day."

New Year's Day?

I almost drop the potato masher. That's nearly a month. And considering the fact that we've barely spoken to each other—let alone spent time living under the same roof—since Mom died...this could get interesting.

And by *interesting*, I mean bad.

After dinner, Macie curls up on the couch with Dad and a Christmas storybook, the two of them practically giddy with holiday glee. When Dad finishes reading, Macie tumbles upstairs with Grams to get ready for bed, leaving me alone with Dad for the first time in what feels like forever.

"What made you come? After you forgot about us on Thanksgiving and everything, I mean." The question leaps out of my mouth with more bravado than I knew I had in me. Even from my spot across the room, I can see Dad flinch. "Sorry." I shrug. "Just curious."

Dad's eyes shrink into slits, and he drops his head. "I'm doing the best I can, Olive. Why can't you at least try to see things from my perspective?"

"I *am* trying." I puff out a sigh and tug on a piece of hair. "But it's hard knowing that half the time you never answer my texts until the next day. It's hard knowing that you've built this new life for yourself in a hobbit-sized apartment when you could be here with us."

Dad rests his elbows on his knees and pinches the bridge of his nose. "You're right. But it's also hard knowing my oldest daughter would rather live halfway around the globe than spend time with the only parent she has. It's hard knowing that she's sitting over here resenting me when I'm trying my best to make things work out well for all of us."

I wince. "Sorry, Dad."

He waves a hand in the air, as if dismissing my apology like it's nothing more than a pesky fly.

"No, I mean really." I stand and cross the room, but something keeps me from sitting next to him. "I'm sorry. I don't do change well."

He offers a sheepish smile. "Guess you got that from me."

A small bit of the hard casing around my heart melts away, and I return his smile before sitting on the other end of the couch. "Grams does a good job decorating, doesn't she?"

Dad nods. "Now I know who your mother learned it from." He props his chin on one hand as he leans his elbow on his knee, and his gaze wanders around the room before landing on the Christmas tree.

"I don't see the ornament."

"Ornament?" A shiver tickles the base of my neck as Dad stands and takes a step toward the tree.

"One from your mom. You helped her pick it out years ago—Bonnie always said it was her favorite." Dad crosses the room and circles the tree. "That's funny."

My heart flutters in my chest, and I stay frozen in place on Gramma's couch. "What—what did it look like?"

"It was blown glass." Dad forms a circle with his hands. "With a little present dangling inside."

"Oh—uh." My heart jumps so high it practically sticks in my throat. "Actually..."

Dad's face falls. "Did she decide not to hang it this year?"

"Kind of." I bite my lip and close my eyes for a second. If the already-pained frown on Dad's face is anything to go by, he isn't going to like what I have to say next. "Macie actually—I mean, when we were decorating the tree, she kind of...I wasn't holding on to it very tight. She—it dropped."

"You mean…you broke it?" Dad's thin voice could belong to a whining toddler.

I nod.

"You couldn't fix it?"

"It's glass, Dad. It shattered into a million pieces." I reach into my sweater pocket and finger the glass present, but I don't dare pull it out and show him.

"And you threw them all out?"

I start to pull out the chipped piece of glass, but something tells me showing it to Dad won't make this mess any better. "I feel terrible about it. We all do."

Dad stays silent, his face black as coal. Which is probably what I'd be getting in my stocking this year, if Santa Claus *did* exist. As it is, I don't even have a stocking to hang. It's probably packed away somewhere in Dad's new apartment. *If* he didn't already donate our Christmas stuff to the Salvation Army.

"Dad?" I rise from the couch and take a step toward him as he rubs a hand over a day's worth of stubble on his chin. "It's only an ornament."

"Right. Of course, it is." His Adam's apple bobs as he swallows, and he brushes past me on his way to the doorway. "I'm going to turn in for the night. See you tomorrow?"

"Tomorrow." I follow Dad with my eyes as he heads upstairs, my heart throbbing with his every step.

Chapter Eight

THE NEXT MORNING, JAZZ AND I are bent over our schoolwork at Gramma's dining room table when Dad tumbles downstairs, rubbing at puffy red eyes. His face seems gray as he crosses over to the kitchen, but his expression brightens when he glances our way.

"You must be Jazz." His mouth crimps into a smile, and he grabs the overripe banana Grams tried to foist off on me earlier this morning. "I've heard a lot about you."

"Only the good stuff, of course." I flash a grin at Jazz, who responds with a crinkle-nosed smile.

"Nice to meet you, Mr. Galloway." She holds onto the table as she climbs to her feet, then takes a step forward and sticks out her hand for Dad to shake.

"Just call me Alex." Dad's head bobs up and down as he gives Jazz a once-over, and his face pales when his eyes reach her prosthetic leg. "Great to finally meet you."

"Same here." Jazz pumps Dad's hand up and down, then collapses back into her chair. "Olive says you teach at Harvard. Any chance you're a math professor? This quiz is killing me."

Dad chuckles and peels his banana. "Nope. Psychology. Besides, if you two want to do school online, you have to actually *do school.*"

"Rats." Jazz pooches out her lip and waves goodbye as Dad backs out of the room.

"Have a good day." His voice floats down the hall, and the front door slams a few moments later.

"He seems cool." Jazz's eyes wander over to the now-empty doorway.

"I guess." Last night's awkwardness plays on fast-forward across my brain and I shrug, But...I guess, to someone who never even knew her father, Dad would seem pretty great. "I'm luckier than I think, most of the time."

"We all are." Jazz ducks her head and returns to her quiz, but I sit for a while, staring at nothing as her words run through my head.

She's right, you know. People can always stand to be more grateful. Especially you. The little voice in my head laughs, and I sigh. Why does my conscience have to be so *right*?

My pocket dings with a text right after I finish my own test. Jazz is still buried up to her nose in papers and eraser crumbs, so I dig my phone out and check my notifications.

"Brander wants us to call him."

"Huh?" Jazz shakes her head and rubs her eyes. "Isn't he in school?"

"Guess not." A tremor runs through my gut, and I tap my fingers as I wait for Jazz to finish her quiz before dialing Brander and putting the phone on speaker.

"Hey." He answers on the first ring. "Is this an okay time?"

"It's fine. But aren't you supposed to be in school?" Jazz quirks an eyebrow toward the phone.

"That's kind of what this is about."

"You're going on tour, aren't you?" I don't need to hear Brander's response. The hesitation on his end is answer enough.

"It's a really big one," he finally says. "With all kinds of major-name artists. The opener's wife went into labor two months early, and they really, really need someone to replace him."

"Will you get to hang out with the other artists?" Jazz perks up. "Can you get me one of their CDs?"

Brander laughs. "Of course. Though I don't know how much I'll really be hanging out with them."

"Doesn't matter." Jazz shakes her head and grins. "This is too cool."

"When do you leave?" The words are dry in my throat. So much for listening to Brander lead worship at the Christmas Eve service. Exchanging gifts together. Not that I was even planning on buying him anything, but still. It was a nice idea.

"Mike booked me a red eye out of Kahului tomorrow evening."

"So soon?" Jazz and I say it at the same time, then giggle, though my laugh feels awfully forced.

"I know." Brander half-groans. "That's partly why I'm calling. I'd really like to do something fun before I head out. Are you guys up for playing hooky tomorrow?"

"We'll make it work, right, Jazz?" She nods. "When were you thinking?"

We decide on a time to meet up, and Brander offers to pick Jazz up at Ruby's before coming over to get me. "I'll let you get back to your work. See ya."

We say goodbye and hang up before Jazz lets out a squeal that could pierce a deaf person's eardrums.

"Isn't this the coolest? Brander's all grown up and ready to go out on tour." Her eyes spark as she opens her biology textbook.

I nod slowly, then faster as I let the idea sink in. Brander—our own Brander—is going on a national tour with some of the biggest names in Christian music. No matter how much I wish he was staying in Maui for the holiday, that can't dampen the seed of excitement blooming in my heart. This has been Brander's dream for as long as I've known him.

And I *will* be happy for him—no matter how much it hurts.

Brander shows up right on time the next day, convertible top down and Jazz settled in the front seat. I climb in back to a soundtrack of "Mele Kalikimaka"—I think I have it memorized by now— and buckle my seatbelt before Brander zips off down the road.

"Where are we going?" I rub my hands over my

bare arms—the air is a little nippy this morning—as Brander turns a corner.

"One of my favorite places on the island."

"Cool." I lean back against the seat and close my eyes, picturing a deserted beach with a lone palm tree by the shore or a rainforest filled with tropical birds.

And then, only a few minutes later, the car slows. I open my eyes.

Everything I'd imagined about Brander's special place falls away as I blink up at the multi-story mass of modern architecture that is the Delacroix mansion.

I haven't been over to Brander's place much—once, to be exact—and I still remember how out of place I felt amid the opulent landscaping and plush, island-inspired decor. I cock my head at Brander as he pulls into a garage around the side of the house. "Your favorite place on the island is your house?"

Brander nods. "I got super homesick when I was in Nashville. It's so weird to be leaving again. Already. Besides," he turns to Jazz, "I have a feeling Olive will want to see the Christmas decorations."

My heart perks up a bit at the thought of an entire mansion filled with Christmassy

wondrousness, and a spring sneaks into my step as Brander ushers me and Jazz inside. Besides, coming in through the garage is a lot less intimidating than entering through the giant paneled French doors out front. I follow Brander and Jazz past a pantry and a strangely normal-looking laundry room before stepping into the Delacroixs' luxe, open-air living room.

Christmas carols float out from speakers hidden somewhere in the teakwood paneling, and a double-decker Christmas tree stands proudly in the center of the space. I can't keep my mouth from dropping open—especially when I catch sight of an oversized nativity display in a far corner—and Brander laughs. "I knew you'd like it."

"It's amazing." My voice is small as I turn in a circle to absorb the beauty of the room. "Mom would be going crazy right now."

We settle onto a couch and spend the rest of the morning talking and, in my case, ogling the decorations.

By lunchtime, my pocket has buzzed half a dozen times, so I pull it out and give my notifications a scan while I'm in the bathroom. Six texts, all from Dad, asking when I'm planning on coming back to Gramma's place.

Don't know. Why?

Dad doesn't respond, so I shrug and head out to join Brander and Jazz for lunch on the terraced patio. Even though part of me aches to know that this is the last time I'll see Brander for who-knows-how-long, the rest of the afternoon still manages to fill my heart with light and joy.

It's only after we drop Jazz off at Ruby's place, when Brander walks me to the door at Gramma's place, that a lump blossoms in my stomach.

"Don't be sad." Brander's brow pinches. "The tour only lasts until the start of the New Year. And wait—" He jogs back to his car and returns a few seconds later, holding a red-and-green striped bag brimming with sparkly white tissue. "This is for you."

"You didn't have to get me a present." Heat crawls up my cheeks as I accept the package.

"I know. But I wanted to." He reaches up to pat his cowlick. "You can't open it until Christmas Day, though."

"You seriously expect me to wait that long?" I squish my eyes half-shut in a mock glare.

Brander laughs. "Christmas Eve, then."

I lift a shoulder. "Fair enough."

A twinkle shines in Brander's eyes, and he gives

me a quick squeeze before dashing down the front steps. "Aloha, Olive."

"Aloha." I raise my hand in a wave as Brander turns and walks backward toward his car.

And even though my heart floods with melancholy the moment he hops inside and starts up the engine, I can't ignore the flicker of excitement that I feel for him. He's living his dream—and that has to be the very best Christmas present a person could ever get.

Chapter Nine

"WHAT DO YOU HAVE TO SAY for yourself?" Dad stands, arms crossed, in the front entryway. "Didn't you get my texts? And what were you *doing?*"

"Huh?" I blink at Dad and set down the gift bag Brander gave me. "Didn't Grams tell you? Today's Brander's last day on the island. I had to say goodbye."

"And Brander is—who? Your boyfriend?" Dad waves a hand in the air, then brings it to his face and pinches the bridge of his nose. "How long have you been together?"

"Dad." I make a move to inch down the hall past him, but he blocks me. "Brander is Jazz's friend. And mine. But he's not, like, my boyfriend."

Dad narrows his eyes at me and folds his arms over his rumpled button-down shirt. "Does Bonnie know about all of this?"

"Of course. Grams has known Brander way longer than I have."

"What are you two saying about me?" Footsteps

come from above, and Gramma appears at the upstairs landing.

I breathe a great sigh and motion to her. "Dad thinks Brander and I have some kind of secret romance going on." I turn to Dad and shake my head at him. "Don't you remember me telling you about Brander? He's the one who helped raise the money for Jazz's leg."

"Yes, but…" Dad's still pinching his nose. His face is a freaky shade of

flamingo pink. "I didn't realize you two were getting physical."

"Physical?" I throw both hands into the air. "We've never hugged for longer than a millisecond. And—wait. Were you spying on us?"

Dad stiffens. "I have every right to check up on my daughter's behavior. Especially when she's skipping school to go off with some young man."

"Grams? Help?" My gaze crawls over to Gramma, who seems to have taken a sudden interest in straightening all of the photos on the wall.

She lifts her head and sighs, then clambers down the rest of the stairs to stand beside Dad. "Alex, I've known Brander since he was in the church nursery." Dad seems to relax a bit, so Gramma opens her mouth again. "He's a kind and godly young man with only the purest intentions."

"He doesn't want to date until he finds someone to marry, Dad." I raise an eyebrow. "Until then, he just wants to be a friend."

Dad harrumphs.

"Olive's right." Gramma pats Dad's rigid shoulder. "Brander grew up leading worship for the youth group, and he's heading out tonight on a national Christian music tour. Nothing to be afraid of."

Dad's color fades to a more natural shade of red, but his gaze still seems uncertain. "Even if this young man is honorable, that doesn't excuse Olive's actions."

"But what did I *do*?" I plant my hands on my hips and look from Dad to Gramma. If I've learned one thing since I've been here, it's that Grams runs a tight ship. If I did something wrong, she'd be the first to let me know.

"You left the house—on a school day—without my knowledge. Not only did you neglect your studies, but you completely ignored my texts."

"Yeah. And you've never ignored any of mine." The words spew from my mouth like a team of flying reindeer. Dad's color rises again, and I wince. "Sorry."

"How dare you—"

"Take it easy, Alex." Gramma tugs on Dad's hand and gives her head a shake.

I shoot her my most thankful expression. "Dad, I'm sorry I didn't answer your texts today. I told Gramma Brander was picking me up, and I never check in with her when I go somewhere. I didn't think—"

"Fine. You don't need to explain." Dad flaps a hand in the air and turns to go upstairs. "But next time, please keep me informed. Okay?"

Because you've been so good at doing that with me. I bite down on my tongue with every bit of resolve I have to avoid uttering that thought out loud. Instead, I wait until Dad has disappeared upstairs, then turn to Gramma. "What's going on with him?"

She dips her chin. "He's been out of sorts all morning. I think he's having a hard time here. Too many memories of your mother." Her usually omnipresent smile gives way to a bittersweet expression. "This is a hard season—for all of us."

Grams steps forward and sweeps me into a hug, but I barely feel it as numbness spreads over me. She releases me, but I don't offer another word before trudging into the living room.

Ignoring the tree—and one empty branch in particular—I shuffle across the floor and crawl into the seat by the window.

I stare out at the surf, tune my ear to the sound of the crashing waves, and let it all wash over me. If only it could cleanse me. Soothe me. Take me back to a time when all was good. A time *Before.*

"Olive?" A chubby hand paws at my hair, coaxing me to emerge from my fitful doze.

"What's up?" I roll over and squint at Macie. Her round face is splashed with bits of golden late-afternoon sunlight, her chin is puckered, and her cocoa-colored eyes are swirled with milky tears.

"Daddy's mad." Macie crawls onto the loveseat next to me and buries her head in my shoulder.

"Really?" I sigh. "Figures."

"I don't even know what I did." She sniffs and swipes at her nose. "But he's mad that I was being a lummox. I don't even know what that *means.*"

I roll my eyes at Dad's ridiculous Harvard-level vocabulary, then wrap an arm around Macie. "It's not your fault. He was already upset because of something I did."

"That's not true." She shakes her head. "He's mad because I'm a lummox. I heard him say so to Grammy. That I broke that ornament so I'm a foolish lummox."

"Oh. The *ornament*."

"Why does that make it different?" Macie stares at me, her eyebrows quirked.

I bite my lip. After the tree-trimming accident left a tiny part of Gramma's heart shattered, I didn't figure there was any point in explaining the ornament's significance to Macie. But maybe... "It was one of Gramma's favorite ornaments. And it was special to Dad too. He's a little upset that it's not hanging on the tree this year."

"Why can't we make them a new special ornament?" Macie plucks at her T-shirt.

"That's a sweet idea, but it's not that—" Wait. I pull the salvaged glass present from my pocket.

Maybe this is why I've been keeping it close all this time.

"Let's get to work."

One hour, half a string of twine, and a few dozen handfuls of sparkling beads later, Macie holds our creation up to the light.

Several inches of carefully strung beads and shards of seagrass spin and sparkle in the light like a chain of ice crystals, at the end of which hangs the present. I tie the other end of the string to an ornament hook, then hand it to Macie. "Don't drop it." I place a hand on her back as we cross the room to the Christmas tree.

"Hang it right there, and don't tell anyone. Let's make it a surprise." I point to the empty branch I've been eyeing ever since I dropped the ornament. Macie nods, and I hold my breath as she slips the ornament hook onto the fake-pine bough.

Gramma's old CD turntable clunks, ushering in a new disc, and Amy Grant bursts out with a high-speed rendition of "Jingle Bells."

Macie backs away from the tree and grins, then shimmies her hands and kicks up her heels before dancing all around the room. "Come on!" She throws her arms out toward me, and I cross over to join her.

Laughter bubbles in my ear as I pick Macie up and spin in a quick circle before setting her down again. Sleigh bells spill from Gramma's speaker, and I dance along with the rhythm as Macie bounces at my side.

I steer her farther away from the tree as a laugh, one that's pure and light and feather-soft, blooms in my chest. Letting go of Macie, I spin in a slow, lazy circle as salted sea air wraps me in a warm embrace. The porcelain nativity on the end table sparkles in the sunlight. Even though it's not as familiar as Mom's quirky needle-felted set, the arrangement still captures the beautiful mystery of the season.

Macie grabs my hand and squeezes, and I squeeze back. Just the way Mom used to do with me. The thought smarts at first—what I wouldn't give to be squeezing *Mom's* hand right now—but then Macie giggles, and the sound of her voice smooths a sweet, velvety balm over my heart.

So we dance together, moving back and forth and side-to-side in rhythm with the carol. The music swells, filling my ears. My bones. My heart.

The ornament winks at me from its place on the tree, and I wink back. The song about jingle bells and open sleigh rides fades away, until the symphony playing in my chest is all I can hear.

So I waltz over to the CD player, flip it off, and sing the words that are in my heart. Macie stares at me like I've finally cracked, but I can't stop as words from that carol—the one that unlocked the memory of that day Mom and I bought Gramma's ornament—pour from my soul.

O morning stars, together, proclaim the holy birth,
And praises sing to God, the King,
and peace to men on earth.

Light catches my eye, and I turn back to the tree. My gaze falls from Gramma's glittery starfish tree topper to the new ornament, which sparkles and twinkles in the light. And in that moment, the shining light looks a little bit like the glow of that miraculous star in the Bible. The one that led a normal person like me to a manger filled with God's greatest gift to all mankind.

I keep singing, and as I do, I lift my hand and blow a kiss toward Heaven.

And peace to men on earth.

Chapter Ten

MY AFTERNOON CRAFTING SESSION MIGHT HAVE fixed things with Macie, but my heart still pinches the next time Dad and I cross paths—way too soon for my own personal taste.

"Olive?" Dad's gaze locks with mine from across the dinner table later that night. "Would you give the blessing?"

"Um. Sure." I shrug and bow my head. Grams isn't too big on long, formal prayers. Usually we talk to God quietly, on our own terms, or say a quick blessing out loud before we eat. But Dad's always been a little more structured. Maybe because he was raised Catholic, maybe because he spends most of his days surrounded by stodgy psychology nerds.

Whatever the reason, something tells me that this "blessing" is a test. And I don't only *want* to pass. I have to.

I bow my head, take a deep breath, and start by thanking God for the meal. "Please bless the hands that prepared it, and..." my tongue falters over the rest of my words, and I start again. "God, be with us today and every day. Remind us what Christmas is really about. Be with us all and take good care of Mom. Amen."

I raise my head.

Dad's gaze is hard and cold. Solid.

I blew it.

Then he nods, and a crack in the iron shield surrounding his gaze appears. "Well said." He dips his head and shoves a forkful of salad into his mouth.

Gramma meets my gaze and nods, and I relax back against my chair. Maybe I can corner Dad after dinner. Get him to talk. Apologize for every rough word I've spoken during these past six months.

Sure, they needed to be said.

But was it my place to get down on him like I did?

Much as I hate to do it, I'm going to have to suck up my pride and have a talk with him. Sooner, rather than later.

Best laid plans and all that...

Shaking my head, I watch from my perch on the

loveseat later that night as Dad and Macie start on their third round of Candyland. I could join in, but I know they need this time together.

Earlier, I overheard Macie ask Dad what a lummox was—and Dad spent about ten minutes apologizing for what Macie overheard him say to Gramma. Now, Macie seems fine, but Dad is acting extra uncomfortable. Best to let them have this time together to clear the air.

Besides, Macie has always been a daddy's girl—and Dad has been wrapped around her chubby little finger since day one. Why should I intrude on their bonding time?

Instead, I twirl my necklace around my fingers and stare at the newest addition to the Christmas tree. No one has noticed it yet, and for some reason, I feel weird pointing it out. Better to let Dad and Grams find it on their own.

Finally, after what must be a million trips through the peppermint forest and molasses swamp, Dad half-carries a drowsy Macie up to bed.

"I thought they'd never stop." I sigh as they leave the room, then glance over at Gramma, who has been stringing beads all evening. "If I have to hear one more thing about gumdrops or gingerbread, I think I'll be sick."

Gramma chuckles, but her expression sobers as she looks up at me. "Is it hard for you?"

"To listen to them ramble about the lollypop palace?" I shrug. "Not the easiest thing in the world."

"No. I mean seeing them together. Having such fun." Gramma raises an eyebrow, and I sit up straighter against the saggy back of the loveseat.

"I still don't get it." I twist my necklace tighter around my pinky. What do I care, seeing Dad and Macie yuck it up all day? I'm happy for them—for Macie.

"Don't play pretend." Gramma lays her work aside and crosses the room to sit next to me. "You're smart enough to know what I mean."

I blink up at Grams and widen my eyes enough to feign innocence. "What *do* you mean?"

"You tell me." Gramma's normally gentle gaze crystallizes into something more severe.

"I'm not a mind reader." I narrow my eyes at Gramma, but one tilt of her chin brings me to submission. "You're asking how it feels to know that they're so happy. To see them carrying on like they did—*Before*. When Mom is...gone."

Gramma nods.

"It stinks."

"I figured you might say that." Gramma lays one hand on my knee. "You know your father loves you. Right?"

I turn to face Grams head-on. "How can you say that? He and I are constantly at each other's throats."

"Might I object to that?" A dark, heavy voice comes from the doorway, and a shiver rattles my core.

"Dad." I drag my head up so I can meet his gaze. "I didn't mean to—"

Dad gives me a look louder than any words he's ever spoken to me. One that says *save your breath*.

I clamp my mouth shut.

"Olive, I have been the worst possible embodiment of a paternal figure an adolescent girl could ask for in these present circumstances." Dad spreads his hands, almost as if to...make peace. "It would do me well to come to you in want of forgiveness. And, perhaps, a revitalization of our relationship."

"Huh?" That's my line.

"English, Alex." Gramma waves a hand at Dad, and he blinks at her.

"It's okay, Grams. He can talk like someone from

Pride and Prejudice if it makes him feel better. I just don't get it—why are you apologizing, Dad? I've been a major jerk for way too long."

"As have I." Dad sits on the couch across the room and props his elbows on his knees, clasping his hands beneath his chin. "Whether you went about it in the right way or not, you had a point today, Olive. A strong one. Why should I expect you to respond to my texts when I've been missing in action for the better part of this year?"

"Dad, wait."

"No." Dad gets to his feet and stands, as if to pace, but I'm too fast for him. I jump from the couch and leap across the room before closing my arms around his narrow frame. And all of a sudden, I'm hugging my dad.

We didn't hug when he showed up on Gramma's doorstep, or when I left for Maui this fall. I don't even think we hugged at Mom's funeral.

But for whatever reason—today, right now—I'm hugging my dad.

His arms are warm and strong around me, and my head fits on his shoulder almost the same as it used to when I was little. I tighten my grip around him and breathe in deep, his shirt smelling a little like Dad, a bit like Gramma's plumeria laundry detergent, and a lot like...*home.*

A handful of tissues and three oversized mugs of hot cocoa later, it happens.

Gramma's gaze lands on the Christmas tree—one newly-decorated branch, in particular—and her eyes seem to double in size.

She climbs to her feet and tiptoes over to examine the tree, moving softly. Swiftly. Like a marionette controlled by invisible threads. "Is that—no." Gramma reaches out and fingers the present, and her breath comes out in a whoosh. "It is."

I raise my mug to hide my expression as Gramma turns back toward me and Dad. "Look, Alex." Her words are hushed—no chance of waking Macie—but they brim with excitement, nonetheless.

"What?" Dad sets his mug on the coffee table and joins Gramma beside the tree. "Is that what I think—"

Gramma nods. "I thought the entire thing had shattered, but...Olive? You wouldn't know anything about this, would you?" A tear slips out from between Gram's feathery lashes.

"Must be Christmas magic." I shrug and take another sip of cocoa.

Magic.

And maybe it really is.

Not the Santa-and-sleigh-bells kind of magic, but the kind Jazz is always talking about. The magic of a Savior come to earth as a baby to redeem the world. The magic of a restored relationship, of a broken family made a tiny bit more whole.

Chapter Eleven

SOMEHOW, THE REST OF THE CHRISTMAS season manages to fly by at the speed of a team of supersonic reindeer. Present-shopping, cookie-making, and carol-singing all weave together to replace my tiffs with Dad. Brander and I talk at least once a week, and Jazz and I also low-key stalk his social media to find pictures of him hanging out with the members of some of our favorite bands.

And then, all of a sudden, I open my eyes one morning, peer at the clock, and—

"It's Christmas Eve!" Macie lets out a bellow that makes her sound like a cross between a humpback whale and an elephant, then launches herself onto my bed. "Get up quick. It's almost time for Santa Claus to come."

"What? It's only eight in the morning. Santa won't be here for *hours*. And when he does come, you'll be asleep." I roll over in bed and come nose-to-nose with Macie. "But it *is* almost time for something else."

Macie cocks her head and stares at me for a

second before her eyes light. "Breakfast! Grammy said she was going to make her special cinnamon rolls." She tumbles off my bed and onto the ground, then springs to her feet and dashes out the door, still dressed in her reindeer-print footie pajamas.

While Macie and Grams clatter around down in the kitchen, no doubt rousing Dad from his slumber, I yawn and cross over to the closet to find an outfit. It might be Christmas Eve, but something tells me that, even if I'd packed them, my usual cozy elf sweater and jeans won't cut it in this Hawaiian heatwave.

A tank top and shorts it is, and I rush through the rest of my morning routine before heading downstairs to join the others.

When I step into the living room, the present ornament winks at me in the midmorning light, and Macie dashes over to join me. "Look." She raises on tippy toes to whisper in my ear. "Mommy's ornament is smiling at us."

I pat Macie's curls and follow her to the dining table, which is festively trimmed with a fake-pine centerpiece and red-and-white striped napkins. We're about to sit down to a late breakfast when someone raps on the front door.

"Now, who could that be?" Gramma's eyes light, and she waggles her brows at Macie. "Why don't you go check, sweetie?"

Macie runs from the table without another word, and it's only a second later when her squeal comes from the hallway. "Jazzie!"

"Oh no." My gut freezes over as I picture the abundance of stocking stuffers—all Jazz's—spread out on Gramma's bedroom floor. I'd been too tired to put them away after wrapping the final one late last night. "Grams, we can't let her walk past your room. Unless we want to spoil the surprise."

Gramma nods, then presses a finger to her lips as Jazz and Macie step through the door to the dining room.

"Looks like I'm right on time." Jazz licks her lips and collapses into the seat next to me. "Merry almost-Christmas, everyone."

"Right back atcha." I grin at Jazz before bowing my head as Dad says a quick prayer.

"Dear Lord Jesus, thank You for coming to earth for us, for giving us this beautiful holiday, and for blessing us with friends to share it with. Let us never forget the reason for our celebration, and please be with each of us on this beautiful day. Amen."

After that, it's a wild free-for-all to see who can eat the most of Gramma's gooey, cream cheese-frosted cinnamon rolls. Jazz, Dad, and Macie all make a good show of it, but I tap out after my second one and can't eat a bite the whole rest of the day.

"You sure you don't want a snack before church?" Jazz waves a bag of sweet Maui onion potato chips in my face as I tie the sash of my red Christmas dress in a bow.

"No way." I wave the chips away and grimace at my reflection in the mirror. "I should never have let Grams go shopping for me. I look like a red velvet cupcake."

"What's wrong with that? Cupcakes are cute." Jazz's smile falters, and she grimaces down at her own outfit, a sparkly white maxi dress that barely hits her mid-calf. "At least you're not growing out of yours."

"It's not bad."

"It shows off more of my leg this way." She grimaces.

"So?"

Jazz shrugs. "I've never had a peg leg for Christmas before."

"Oh. Yeah." A bundle of sadness threatens to come loose in my heart, but I take a deep breath and slap a smile on my face. "Then why don't we celebrate it?"

"Huh?" Jazz crinkles her nose. "Celebrate my prosthesis?"

"Why not? People make such a big deal about baby's first Christmas—why not your leg's first Christmas?"

"Because that's *weird*."

I shake my head and jog to the bedroom door. "No it's not. You'll see."

I dash to Gramma's craft closet across the hall and grab a sparkly, red-and-green bow. "Here." I hold it out to Jazz. "Tie it around the metal rod."

"And *why* would I do that?" Jazz stares at the ribbon, her usually soft gaze hard as ice.

"I dunno. I guess...I thought maybe you'd—"

"Nah. Not today." Jazz's face droops, and she tosses the ribbon on the bed.

"You doing okay?" I throw an arm around her.

"I've tried three times today to call my mom at rehab. She's never in her room." Tears fill Jazz's eyes. "I just wanted to...wish her a merry Christmas, you know?"

"I know." What I wouldn't give for one minute with Mom—to sing a carol with her and give her a hug? To smell her special nutmeg-and-chestnuts Christmas perfume?

"Sorry." Jazz ducks her head. "I forget you're in the same boat."

A balmy breeze floats through the open window, sending a few stray tendrils of hair floating around my face. By the time the wind calms down, Jazz's eyes have regained a bit of their spark. "I'll make you a deal." She picks up the ribbon and grins at it. "I'll wear a Christmas-bow anklet if you do."

"What?" I almost laugh, then catch myself when Jazz's gaze deepens. "You're serious?"

"Yep."

"Fine." I roll my eyes and grab a pair of scissors from my desk. In a matter of minutes, I'm helping Jazz down the last trio of stairs to join the others around the tree in the living room, a jaunty bow flopping against my ankle the whole way.

"Is it finally time to go?" Macie jumps up and down as Jazz and I appear in the doorway, and I nod.

"But first, let's do our elf thing." My eyes flick over

to Grams, who nods. I grab Macie's hand before jogging down the hall to Gramma's room. We dump a last armful of stocking stuffers into Jazz's hand-decorated Santa sack—compliments of Gramma—then carry the bag down the hall to the living room.

"What's that?" Jazz giggles as we appear, Macie nearly staggering under the weight of the overstuffed sack.

"It's your Christmas." Macie drops it with a thunk and stands with her shoulders back, chest puffed out. "We're your Christmas elves. But you have to wait and open it tomorrow or else Santa will never, ever bring you presents again."

"That's cool, but seriously. What is it?" Jazz takes a step forward and gives the bag a cautious poke.

"It's yours." I waggle my brows at Jazz. "I know you're into the real reason for the season and all that stuff, but no one deserves to get up on Christmas morning without a stocking to open."

"You mean—it's *all* for me? That's an awfully big stocking." Jazz's mouth forms a perfect circle. "You shouldn't have."

"But it was fun." Macie bounces on her heels, and her curls shimmy atop her head. "Now can we go to church? I want to sing Christmas carols."

So that's exactly what we do.

Late that night, after Jazz has gone home—oversized Santa sack in tow—and Macie has been nestled all snug in her bed, I help Dad and Gramma stage the picture-perfect visit from Santa, complete with a half-empty glass of milk and a note from the jolly old fellow himself.

At the last second, I add a PS to the note—*Don't ever forget that the real reason for the season is more than presents. It's about baby Jesus and His gift to all of us. These gifts from me are just the icing on your sugar cookie.* Because Jazz is right, and I'm starting to see what she means. That Christmas really is about *more*.

But gifts can be fun too. Especially the one I'm about to open.

I grab the luxury-wrapped package from Brander before plopping on the couch and texting him.

You said I could open it on Christmas Eve, so here goes.

He doesn't answer—probably resting after the tour's Christmas Eve spectacular in Washington, D.C. I reach into the bag, past three layers of glimmering tissue, and pull out...a calendar?

I snort. What did I expect—another necklace, like the one he got me after we raised the money for Jazz's leg? He's a guy. Of course he'd come up with something dorky like a—a *pineapple* calendar.

Except it's not just a calendar.

There's something taped to the front.

I lean closer into the light from the Christmas tree and scan the peppermint-striped sticky note attached to the cover.

Merry Christmas, Olive! I wish I could be in Maui to celebrate with you in person, but I know I'll be home soon. And when I am...brace yourself. Take a look inside to see for yourself.

That's it—no signature, nothing else. And what does he mean, see for myself?

I flip to the first page, and a giggle slips out. There's more of his slanted scrawl, filling a smattering of boxes across the month's span.

Brander comes back from tour, reads the first one. Then, a few squares later: *Drive the road to Hana.* A week after that is a day devoted to sampling shave ice around the island.

My heart flutters a bit, and I squint in the candlelight to read a note at the bottom of the page. *I've really missed hanging out with you and Jazz since I've been gone so much. I don't know how long I'll be home for this time, but I can promise we'll make the most of it. Here's to friendship, and to the three musketeers.*

The Three Musketeers.

I like it.

A smile spreads onto my face, and I stay there, curled up on the loveseat, grinning at the Christmas tree, for what feels like forever until Grams pokes her head into the room. "Olive? What are you doing up? It's nearly two o'clock in the morning."

I shrug. "It's the last night I get to enjoy Christmas. Mom used to stay out by our tree all night. I thought—I thought I'd carry on the tradition."

Gramma's eyes glow warm and soft, and she eases onto the couch next to me. "That's a very noble goal, but the tradition isn't yours to carry on. It's mine."

"You mean . . ."

Gramma smiles and nods. "I had no idea she did that too. It's always been my favorite part of this day—staying up all night just to look at the tree. To sit for a while and think. Pray."

"Oh." My voice is thick with love and tears and a million other warring emotions, so I tighten my grip on my calendar, slide off the couch, and head for the door. "See you in the morning, then."

"See you, sweetie." Gramma waves, and something in my heart pinches. It stays that way as I climb upstairs and deposit the calendar on my bed. It stays that way as I change into my pajamas. I start to slide between the sheets of my bed.

And that's when I know. There's no way I'm sleeping tonight. Not in my bed, at least.

I tiptoe back downstairs and slip into the living room. "I know it's your tradition and stuff, and maybe you'd like to keep it that way, but...would you mind some company this year?"

"Of course not." Gramma's smile warms. "I'd like nothing more."

I cross the room and sit next to her, lean my head on her shoulder, and stare at the tree. At one special ornament—a mix of old and new, of bitter and sweet—and somewhere, I can almost hear the angels singing like they did on that one sacred, silent night.

Except, this time, Mom's voice is part of the heavenly chorus.

Merry Christmas, sweet girl.

I stare up at the ceiling, eyes suddenly wet.

Merry Christmas, Mom.

Merry Christmas...everyone.

Author's Note

Ah…Christmas.

It's the most wonderful time of the year, isn't it?

Ever since I was little, I've felt the joy and magic of the season deep in my soul. So, after Book Two in the *Tradewinds* trilogy came to a close on Thanksgiving, I knew a Hawaiian-style Christmas celebration was in store for Olive, Jazz, Brander, and the rest of the gang.

Writing this little novella was honestly one of the highest points of my career as a writer thus far. Every chapter brought me so much joy, and I had fun dropping in as many references to family traditions, Christmas carols, and Christmas icons as I could.

In case you're wondering…*yes.*

Outrageous stockings, pre-Christmas "secret Santa" gift-giving, and extreme decorating (we've been known to go as far as decorating our bathrooms with fresh greenery) have been—and continue to be—an integral part of my holidays.

Like Olive, I oftentimes find myself caught up in the glitz, glamor, and glee of the season. I go a little overboard with my holiday shopping and cookie-baking, and some days I need a "Jazz" to pull me back and remind me why I'm doing what I do.

I need someone to remind me that we only have an opportunity to give presents because of *His presence.* That, though I might enjoy a silent night curled up by the tree, the only night that really matters is the one on which Jesus was born.

Jesus is the reason for the season.

And yes. It's a little cheesy, and downright corny sounding, but *it's true.* Without Jesus, Christmas is nothing more than an overdressed, overstuffed Wednesday (or whatever day it happens to fall on). Without Jesus, we have no hope, no peace, and no joy.

But you know what?

Even though we've plucked one dreary winter day out of thin air and declared that *this is the day* we celebrate God's gift to us, we should be rejoicing every day.

Because Jesus came to the world for you and me—for all of us. He gave us the greatest gift. The gift of *life.* He gave us freedom to live, freedom to rejoice in His presence, and freedom to worship Him for eternity.

So this year, as you drink cocoa and hang

ornaments and listen to Christmas carols, remember…

It's all because of Jesus.

This season, this holiday, this *life* is all because of Him.

He is our best gift, our ultimate treasure, and the best Christmas miracle we could ever ask for. And I'm so, so thankful that He is.

Merry Christmas, friends!

XOXO,
Taylor Bennett

P.S., If you enjoyed this story or any of the books in the *Tradewinds* series, I'd love if you'd consider posting a review on Amazon, Goodreads, Christianbook.com, or other places online. Or, if you'd like to connect with me online, you can do that on Instagram @taylor.bennett.author, Facebook @TaylorBennettAuthor, or my website (taylor--bennett.com). Aloha!

Holiday Macadamia Nut Pie

From the Kitchen of Tutu Bonnie

Though there isn't a mention of this rich, nutty pie in Mele Kalikimaka, Gramma always makes this tropical take on pecan pie for Thanksgiving. I like to think it was such a hit with Olive and Macie that they convinced her to make it again as part of Christmas dinner. I know it's definitely a favorite at my house! (Pro tip: Use any kind of nuts you have on hand...each variety adds its own special quality to this luscious pie.)

WHAT YOU NEED:

1/2 cup sugar

1 1/2 cups corn syrup

1/4 cup butter

3 eggs, slightly beaten

1/2 tsp vanilla

1 cup macadamia nuts

1 pie crust

Whipped cream (homemade is best!)

HOW TO MAKE IT:

1. Preheat oven to 350 and place crust in pie pan.
2. Combine sugar, corn syrup, and butter in a saucepan. Mix well over medium heat and bring to boiling.
3. Once the mixture has reached a boil, pour slowly over beaten eggs, stirring constantly.
4. Mix in vanilla and macadamia nuts, then pour into prepared pie crust.
5. Bake 45 minutes or until firm in center. Serve topped with fresh whipped cream.

Discussion Questions

1.   One of the key themes in *Mele Kalikimaka* is Olive's struggle to accept the newness of Christmas in Hawaii when all she wants is what she had *Before*. Have you ever experienced a holiday that was vastly different than your "normal"? If so, how did you adjust to the change?

2.   Olive, Gramma, Macie, and Dad are all dealing with grief during the Christmas season. Is there a time in your life when you experienced grief during the holidays? How did you handle it?

3.   Olive and Jazz discuss their favorite parts of the Christmas holiday—Olive's memories center around her mom's outrageous stocking creations, while Jazz remembers Christmas Eve service and candy canes. What is one of your favorite Christmastime memories?

4.   When Olive and Brander are talking, Brander hints that his volunteer position at the church's support group could be just as important—or even more so—than his music gig in Nashville. Do you

agree with him? Which of these ministry opportunities do you think has an opportunity to impact more lives?

5. Many scenes in the book center around Christmas traditions or memories. What is one of your favorite Christmas traditions? Will you carry it on with your own family someday?

6. Olive and her dad's relationship is still strained, but things seem more peaceful between them by the end of the book. What do you think caused this shift?

7. Olive likes to think of her mother looking down on the family from Heaven. Do you think our deceased Christian friends and family members can look down on us from Heaven? Why or why not? (Read Hebrews 12:1)

www.ingramcontent.com/pod-product-compliance
Lightning Source LLC
Chambersburg PA
CBHW071838190726
48292CB00005B/1820